SCHOOL
FOR
PRINCES

Stories from the Panchatantra

To Kaavya and Ashwin with love – JG
For Maureen, with thanks for all the back-up! – BW

JANETTA OTTER-BARRY BOOKS

School for Princes copyright © Frances Lincoln Limited 2011
Text copyright © Jamila Gavin 2011
Illustrations copyright © Bee Willey 2011

First published in Great Britain in 2011 and in the USA in 2012 by
Frances Lincoln Children's Books, 4 Torriano Mews,
Torriano Avenue, London NW5 2RZ

www.franceslincoln.com

A catalogue record for this book is available from the British Library.

ISBN 978-1-84507-990-1

Illustrated in pencil, oil pastels, acrylic and Photoshop
Set in Bembo

Printed in Shenzhen, Guangdong, China by C&C Offset Printing in April 2011

1 3 5 7 9 8 6 4 2

SCHOOL FOR PRINCES

Stories from the Panchatantra

by Jamila Gavin

Illustrated by Bee Willey

F

FRANCES LINCOLN
CHILDREN'S BOOKS

An Introduction to The Panchatantra

The Panchatantra is a collection of stories on the art of living well and ruling wisely. These ancient tales have been passed down through the rich oral tradition of storytelling. No one knows who composed them, but traditionally they are attributed to Visnu Sarma, a teacher in the Peacock City of Tamil Nadu in India, who undertook to educate three intransigent princes in only six months.

The Panchatantra is divided into five parts. Panch means 'five' in Sanskrit, and tantra means 'weave'. Hanging from the 'loom' are five frames, or main themes:

Winning Friends
Losing Friends
Loss of Gains
Rash Deeds
The Art of Duplicity

Within the five frames are interwoven numerous instructive tales: stories within stories, developing each of the main themes, with the intention of educating the princes into the art of kingship.

I have chosen five Panchatantra stories – one from each theme – and woven in five original stories of my own in which the princes themselves take part.

I hope, like the princes, readers will gain some wisdom from these ancient texts, even if they never expect to rule a kingdom!

Jamila Gavin

CONTENTS

THE PRINCES WHO WOULDN'T LEARN

There was once a king called Amara Sakti, who had three dreadful sons. They were rude, quarrelsome, and completely uninterested in their education. The people of the kingdom dreaded the day when the king would die and his sons would rule over them.

One day, King Amara Sakti received a distinguished visitor who came bearing gifts for the princes. How ashamed the king felt at the sight of his three sons rolling around in a pitched battle over the presents.

"That's mine!"

"Can't have it!"

"Ouch! You kicked me. That hurt!"

"I do apologise. I don't know where I've gone wrong," sighed the king in despair. "I have given them the best of everything. Yet the more they have, the worse they behave. Does this mean that the more I give my people, the less happy they will be? One day, my sons will rule, and I fear that they won't be fit for the task."

The visitor stroked his chin thoughtfully. "This is not just a problem for your royal self, but for all loving parents. Youth, wealth and power are wonderful things in themselves, but when thrown together carelessly, without thought of the consequences, they bring misery. But I know of a wondrous teacher called Visnu Sarma. Although advanced in years, it is said that he can educate anyone. Consult him."

So Visnu Sarma was summoned.

King Amara Sakti looked doubtful, as a man thin with pilgrimage and abstinence was ushered before him. He wore a single white garment, and his long greying hair was tied into a knot on his head. He carried a staff in one hand, and a bundle of books under his arm.

'Advanced in years?' the king thought glumly, remembering his friend's description. 'This man is positively ancient. How can he control my three wild sons?'

Yet there was a spring in the old man's step, and his black eyes glittered with merriment as he bowed respectfully before his sovereign.

"I used to long for a hundred sons," confided the king, "but I have trouble with only three."

As the teacher heard about the appalling princes, his eyebrows rose and fell like grey billows. "It is better to have one sightless eye than three unruly boys, for at least then there is only one problem," he remarked sympathetically.

"I'm sure they are clever and have talents," despaired the king, "but they just won't use them."

"Ah!" The teacher smiled. "A musician can have the finest bow and, drawn across an instrument, it could create miraculous music. But what good is the bow if the instrument has no strings?"

This was music to the king's ears. "Stay with me," he implored. "Make my boys your instruments; give them the strings of virtues, so that when a bow is put across them they will bring harmony into their lives and the lives of others. Stay twenty years if need be."

Sarma gently shrugged. "I only need six months. In six months, my task will be done."

"Six months?" exclaimed the king scornfully. "Impossible! Why, it takes at least twelve years just to master the science of words and grammar."

"Sire, if in six months I fail to educate your sons, awaken in them the joys of knowledge, bring them to an understanding of their spiritual and royal duties and, above all, open their minds, then you may make me a laughing stock."

The king's first instinct was to throw the man out. But he knew that, despite all the fine teachers who had come and gone, his boys were still ignorant, uninterested and unlettered.

"You see, sire," the old man interrupted the royal thoughts, "your sons' curriculum has been a diet of deadwood: indigestible, blunting their intelligence and dulling their brains. They are not stupid. They just need awakening. I don't need ten years to turn your princes into future kings."

"Very well," replied Amara Sakti. "You have six months. But if this turns out to be an idle boast, you will be thrown out of my kingdom."

"So be it," murmured the old teacher.

▶▶

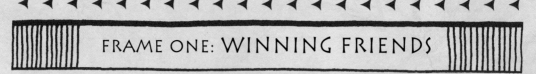
The Fighter Kite

The princes appeared in the school-room the next morning. Vasu, the eldest, stood with an arrogant, languid look, as if the world and the rest of mankind had been designed for his pleasure. He was the first-born boy, the future ruler of most of the kingdom. He expected to get what he wanted at the click of his fingers. He expected total obedience – especially from his younger brothers, whom he bullied mercilessly. Even the court counsellors were afraid of him, though he was just a child.

Ugra was the middle one and, like so many middle children, felt ill done by. People didn't bow and scrape to him as much as they did to Vasu. He hadn't the status of his older brother, nor the sweet novelty of being the youngest. He hated being the second-born. He knew he would always be less powerful than Vasu, and less loved than his younger brother, Ananta.

On the other hand, Ananta knew that his power lay in being the youngest. He was an adorable, chubby, cuddly, spoilt, naughty boy who enchanted his mother, the queen, and his aunts and sisters, nannies and maidservants. They were always stuffing sweetmeats into his mouth, playing with his black curls, and tickling his rather too fat tummy. Courtiers were often to be seen chasing him round the verandas, giving him piggy-backs and tossing him in the air. But beware! If Ananta didn't get what he wanted he would throw a tantrum like a monsoon gale. Yet he was always forgiven. No one could resist his big grin and flashing eyes. The trouble was, he found no reason to stop being a baby.

Smirking before their latest new teacher, the three princes were sure he'd be no better than the rest.

"A half-naked fakir like him can't teach me anything," thought Vasu contemptuously.

"He already despises me," sulked Ugra.

"I'll soon have him wound round my little finger," chortled Ananta.

"We don't feel like learning today," Vasu informed the old teacher. The other two sniggered in agreement.

Old Sarma, sitting cross-legged, his eyes closed in meditation, had been waiting patiently since dawn, and did not immediately respond to the surly voices breaking into his peace of mind.

The boys were annoyed. How dare this old man not greet them! He might be their teacher, but they were princes and expected his instant attention.

Without opening his eyes, Sarma gently requested them to be seated in the lotus postion, and to contemplate their forthcoming day.

"We don't need to waste any time contemplating our day. We know what we want to do," declared Prince Vasu.

"We have been given a fabulous new kite made of silk. We're going to fly it. And you can't stop us!" shouted Ananta.

"Well, go then!" The old man opened his eyes and flashed a smile. "Go, go!" He dismissed them cheerfully. "Fly your kite. I love kite flying. I'll come too."

The boys looked at each other in amazement. Then, with a whoop of joy, they fled the school-room in case their tutor changed his mind.

This royal kite of fine Chinese purple silk and edged with gold was stretched across a bamboo frame. The boys carried it to the top of the watch tower on the highest hill.

"I'm the oldest," announced Prince Vasu, "so I will fly it first."

Soon their kite was soaring on the back of the wind.

"Don't pull so hard!"

"Give it me. I'm best."

"Shut up!"

How the boys squabbled, their voices grating on the air worse than a flock of parakeets!

"Have you ever considered that a kite is freer when it is held by a string, than when it is not?" called their teacher from below. "A kite can only fly when attached to a piece of string, but if freed, would plunge to the ground."

But the princes were in no mood for philosophy.

Over the river, Preeta, a farmer's girl, stood on the low, flat roof of her simple, mud-built house on the edge of the wheatfields, tugging at the string of a small, home-made, paper kite. To the disgust of the princes, her kite rose higher than theirs. They quarrelled even louder.

Ugra had grabbed the string when a sudden change in the wind caught the royal kite and sent it soaring. "Look! It's going even higher than that farm girl's," he chortled with glee. "It's going as high as the sun!"

Then Preeta yelled a warning. "Watch out! The kite-stealer's coming."

He's got a fighter kite!" She began to reel in her kite as fast as she could. She knew what a fighter kite could do; she knew its string was coated with glass and glue and could cut the string of other kites.

But the princes just laughed. "Coward! Loser!" they jeered, certain that it was just a trick. Anyway, no common fighter kite would dare to interfere with the royal kite.

Too late! A menacing, black kite with red-as-blood splashes rose above the trees, guided by a mysterious hand. It was coming their way.

Nearer and nearer it came, its string glinting with glass. The two kites tangled, bucked and kicked. Vasu snatched the string from Ugra and tried desperately to reel in the kite; Ugra grabbed it back. But the more they tussled, the more the fighter kite slashed their string.

Suddenly it was cut. The string trailed free. For a moment the royal kite seemed suspended, then it plunged out of control. With an agonised groan, the princes watched it plummet into the trees, while the fighter kite hovered triumphantly in the sky.

"It's all your fault, you idiot," Vasu raged at his brother.

"No it's not. You're no good at kite flying," bellowed Ugra.

"How shall we get it back?" wailed Ananta.

"We've got to find that fighter kite. How dare he interfere with a royal kite! He must be punished," shouted Vasu.

The princes careered down the tower steps, and made for the woods.

"What is lost is lost. What will be will be. What should be yours will be yours. That is destiny," murmured old Sarma.

All morning they searched, going deep into the wild forest, looking for any sign of the royal kite. They had almost given up with exhaustion, when they heard strange sounds: enticing, magical music seemed to lure them deeper into the forest. The princes followed the sound.

Sitting under a tulip tree was Sarma. How had he got there? The old man was playing a lilting melody on a wooden flute. "Ah ha!" He smiled a serene smile. "I hope you are good climbers."

The princes looked up – and there at the very top, caught in the upper branches, was the royal kite.

"I saw where it came down," said Sarma, "and sat here to keep guard."

Without even a "thank you" to their teacher, the princes began arguing about how to get it down.

"You'll have to do what the doves did when they were caught by the evil fowler," said old Sarma.

"What are you talking about?" scoffed Prince Vasu.

"It's all about having friends," explained Sarma. "Come! Sit here by me and I'll tell you."

The princes sat down sullenly. What else was there to do?

"Let me tell you a story," Sarma murmured.

14

Caught in the Fowler's Net

A task, no matter how hard,
Can be carried through with the help of friends;
So find good friends and,
In finding them, treasure them.

Crow was about to fly towards the city in search of food, when suddenly a bird-catcher, a most evil-looking man, came right up to his tree. With net, club and knotted noose in hand, he looked like Death himself. Snarling at his heels came his dogs, with salivating jaws and bared teeth.

'This man is out to trap me and my fellow birds,' thought Crow, and gave a warning "caw"!

He watched as the fowler spread out his net and scattered grain all around. Then, motioning his dogs to follow, the man hid himself nearby.

"Be careful," Crow warned the other birds. "It's a trick! Don't peck the grain." They listened to him, and didn't take any grain.

Just then, high in the sky, King Dove was flying in search of food. He spotted the scattered grain and, with his whole retinue of doves, eagerly descended.

"Danger!" cawed Crow. "Don't touch it! That grain is a bird-catcher's trick to trap you in his net."

'Huh!' thought King Dove. 'More likely a crow's trick so that he can have the grain all to himself.'

He landed on the ground with all his followers. Greedily, they began to peck, and in no time at all their feet became entangled in the net. They were trapped.

Out sprang the fowler with club in hand, and snarling dogs. He advanced on the doves, his red-shot eyes bulging with glee.

The doves panicked, struggling in vain to get free. Faced with death, King Dove's mind cleared as quickly as a summer mist. "Stay calm!" he urged his followers. "If we work together, we can survive. Do as I say. Each take some net in your beaks, and when I give the signal, flap your wings. Together we'll fly out of his reach."

The doves obeyed instantly and, just as the bird-catcher was nearly upon them, King Dove gave the signal: "Now!"

As one, they all flapped their wings and, though still entangled in the net, rose upwards and out of reach of the leaping dogs. The fowler roared with fury.

The doves, now free, yet still imprisoned, flew across the sky, while below, the fowler gave chase, hoping they would soon become exhausted and come tumbling to earth again. But wise King Dove flew towards rocky hills and dense scrub, and soon it was the fowler, scratched, bruised and exhausted, who gave up.

However, they were not out of danger. King Dove knew they couldn't disentangle themselves from the net without help. He desperately scoured the earth below. Then he remembered Mole.

"Mole is my friend. He lives not far from here. He will help us."

16

Mole was out nibbling around for food when a shadow came between him and the warmth of the sun. He squinted skywards. A giant billowing thing was making straight for him. Terrified at the thought of ending up as someone's supper, Mole scuttled back into his hole underground.

"Mole, Mole! Dear friend!"

Did he know that voice? Mole wondered.

"Mole, Mole! Help!"

How did this creature know his name? Mole feared a trick. If he came out of his hole he was sure he'd be gobbled up.

"Mole! It's your old friend King Dove."

King Dove? Mole hadn't seen King Dove for ages. But how could it be him? That awful creature out there was no dove. Still, the voice sounded familiar, so he crept forward and peeped out of his hole.

King Dove spotted his friend's shiny nose. "Dear Mole, don't be afraid. It is I, King Dove. Help me!"

Mole wriggled out further. Being very short-sighted, all he could make out was a writhing creature on the ground. It seemed to have no single head and no single body, but was made up of many heads and bodies and fluttering feathers.

"Alas, I ignored Crow's warning," explained King Dove, and he told Mole the whole sorry story. "With your sharp teeth, could you gnaw through the net and release us?"

Mole crept closer, and saw that it was indeed King Dove and all his flock trapped in the net. Eager to help, he set about nibbling the net which entangled King Dove's feet. But King Dove stopped him. "No, dear friend! Don't free me first. Free my followers."

Mole was somewhat miffed. "You get into trouble, ask for my help, then tell me to stop. Let me do it my way. After all, you are the king and should be freed first."

"Forgive me, dear Mole. I didn't wish to criticise your efforts but, as king, I must put my people first. If a king sees to the welfare of his citizens, then he can expect their total loyalty in return. Isn't that so?"

"You are a noble monarch," sighed Mole admiringly, and set about releasing the other doves first. Finally, with aching jaws and blunted teeth, he freed them all!

"You see," Sarma said, his eyebrows billowing up and down. "King Dove remembered that the first duty of a king is to his people. Though even kings can be deaf to what they don't want to hear. If only he'd listened to Crow, who was just trying to be a friend. But at least he came to his senses in the face of death, and planned their escape. Of course, it could still have ended badly if it hadn't been for Mole. Eh?"

The princes yawned and nibbled the stalks of grass between their teeth, as if they were bored. "So? What has that got to do with getting our kite back?" drawled Vasu indifferently.

"I'm sure," murmured old Sarma, getting to his feet, "that you young sirs will find a way, especially with the help of a friend!" And he glanced behind him. Preeta, the farmer's girl, was sitting on her haunches listening from a respectful distance. "I'm an old man and no use to you, so I'll be off." And, with a wink of his eye, away he went.

The boys stared up at the beleaguered royal kite, caught at the top of the tree. Far away, a dog was barking, while a rough voice berated it.

"If it please you, sirs," said Preeta, daring to speak. "We'd better do something quickly. The kite-stealer's coming, and he has a fierce dog."

"I'm not letting him get my kite," stormed Vasu.

"Our kite," corrected Ugra.

"Climb the tree, Vasu!" urged Ananta. "You're the tallest."

"I'll stay at the bottom to direct operations," stated Vasu. "Ugra, you climb the tree. Get on with it."

"I can't! I'm afraid of heights," protested Ugra. "What about Ananta? We can both give him a leg up."

"Good idea! Come on, Ananta!" His brothers advanced towards him.

Ananta screamed in protest. "Not me! It would ruin my clothes. Send for the servants!"

"Oh no!" Vasu exclaimed. "That will make us a laughing stock, and people will say that we were too feeble to climb the tree and get it ourselves."

"He's coming," whispered Ugra. The barking dog thundered nearer. The monkeys chattered nervously. "The kite-stealer's coming!"

"I can help," said Preeta.

"You? You're just a girl!" they sneered.

"I love climbing trees," she smiled. "If Your Majesties would agree to bend over near the tree," she gestured towards the two older princes, "then His Gracious Majesty, Prince Ananta, can stand on your backs, and I can climb on his shoulders – with your royal permission of course – and reach that overhanging branch."

"It's worth a try, I suppose," said Vasu. "It's our only hope."

"Must I have her dirty feet on my shoulders?" grimaced Ananta, but his brothers just cried, "Oh, get on with it!"

Vasu and Ugra made a platform of their backs. Preeta helped
Ananta stand on top of them and clasp
the trunk with his arms. Preeta then
climbed on to the royal backs and up
on to Ananta's shoulders. "I'm up!"
she yelled, pulling herself
into the tree. The barking
was horribly close.
"We're not going to
make it." The princes on
the ground looked around,
panic-stricken, for means of
escape. "What shall we do?"
"Climb the tree! Grab my arms." Preeta
reached down and first hauled up Ananta.
"My jacket! My trousers!" wailed Ananta,
slapping Preeta when he was safely in the tree.
"Stop fussing, Ananta!" shouted his brothers.
Ugra then stood on Vasu's shoulders, and
Preeta pulled him to safety. Now there was just Vasu left
on the ground.
The grunting and barking was closer still. Ugra and Ananta
held Preeta's ankles as she leaned right out of the tree,
hanging upside down like a trapeze artist. "Grab my arms!"
Vasu clasped Preeta's arms and they hauled him to safety
just as an evil-looking man crashed through the bushes.
He was carrying a hooked pole, long enough to reach
the top of the tree. His huge dog snarled and leapt all
four paws off the ground, snapping at the children with his
sharp white teeth.
The children scrambled ever higher, tucking in their
feet, and clinging to the branches for dear life.
The kite-stealer glared up at them with fury.

Slowly, with a malignant grin, he lifted the pole. He would shake them out of the tree like mangoes.

"Grab the hook," whispered Preeta. "If we all hang on to it, he won't be able to pull it back. I can tie it to the tree with my veil."

The hook came closer, searching them out. It had almost hooked Ananta's ankle when Preeta shouted, "Now!"

They grabbed the hook. Preeta tore off her veil. She wrapped one end round and round the hook and tied the other end to a branch.

The kite-stealer shook the pole violently, but it held fast.

The sound of a conch horn echoed in the distance. Voices called out, "Masters! Royal sirs! Where are you?"

The kite-stealer let go the pole with a sudden, awful realisation. He had been attacking the king's own sons. Whistling sharply, he made off into the undergrowth with the hound leaping at his heels.

Laughing with relief, the princes began their descent.

"Wait!" cried Preeta. "You're forgetting something." She shinned up, branch by branch, to the top of the tree and released the silken kite.

Sarma and some servants appeared just as the princes leapt to the ground, and Preeta lowered the kite safely into their hands.

"We did it together! Just like King Dove!" they congratulated themselves.

"Not forgetting Preeta, of course," said old Sarma, glancing at the farm girl abandoned in the tree.

"Of course. Yes. We couldn't have done it without Preeta!" said Vasu with unexpected generosity. The princes helped her down and surrounded her, full of admiration. "You shall have a new veil. Six new veils, and silk garments to go with them!" declared Prince Vasu.

"Ah!" murmured old Sarma. The boys had learned their first lesson.

Even princes need friends, just as an ocean needs water.

▸▸

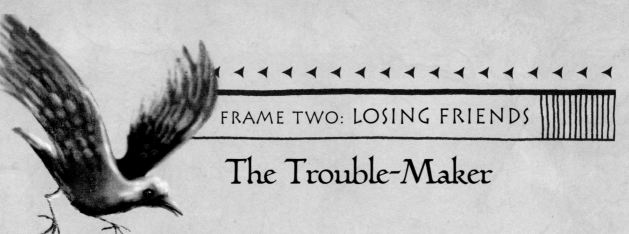

The Trouble-Maker

When Prince Kanu, son of King Bhoja, came to stay from a neighbouring kingdom, he was puzzled. His younger cousins, the three princes, seemed to be enjoying their lessons with their new teacher, Sarma. Unheard of! And what's more, they had a new friend – a mere farm girl called Preeta. In fact, they seemed to relish being with her more than anything.

Being older and taller than his cousins, Prince Kanu was used to their admiration and esteem. He was always the leader in their games, and the centre of attention, and he was used to them doing whatever he told them. So on this visit, he felt put out, and sneered at them for the time they spent sitting round their teacher, Sarma, listening to his stories like little children. And he was even more mocking when they went off in search of Preeta. How they praised this poor little farm girl, who seemed to know everything. It was Preeta this and Preeta that.

Who was this Preeta? thought Kanu bitterly. Why, just a lower-caste nothing – not fit even to walk in their shade.

"Don't know what you see in that dirty girl!" he sneered. "You should be careful. You might catch something."

"Don't be stupid," retorted Vasu.

"Yeh – well you should watch people like that," advised Kanu. "Stick with your own kind – and they should stick with theirs. Otherwise they forget their place. People like that only hang around being your friend for what they can get out of it. After all," he murmured to Vasu when

they were on their own, "one day, you'll be king – that's if one of your brothers doesn't beat you to it. I've heard that there's nothing Ugra would like more than to be king. Ananta too, I imagine," Kanu drawled.

Vasu was horrified. "How dare you talk such rubbish!" he shouted.

"Suit yourself," retorted Kanu. "You're mad to trust Preeta. I wouldn't be surprised if her family encourages the friendship. They must dream of what gains they'll get out of it. Haven't you noticed how she and your brothers are always talking together secretly? Who knows what plots they are hatching. I'd watch my back if I were you."

Alhough Vasu ridiculed Kanu's sly suggestions, he was filled with doubt. The poison had entered his brain. He began to see things differently. What were Preeta and Ugra laughing about? Why were Ugra and Ananta whispering, their arms clasped across each other's shoulders, their heads touching, as if sharing a secret, when they usually fought like cat and dog? And was Ananta only shouting in fun when he declared, "I am the conquering king!" as Preeta galloped off with him on her back, pretending she was a horse carrying a king to war? Could they really be plotting to overthrow him one day?

Vasu had a birthday coming soon and there were to be the usual lavish celebrations. It was Preeta who suggested to Ugra and Ananta that they give Vasu a special birthday surprise. Whenever Vasu was out of the way, they would sit round in a huddle and listen to her ideas. But somehow, they didn't include Kanu. He felt left out and resentful.

One day, Kanu went to the river where Preeta was scrubbing down the buffaloes. For a while, he lounged on a rock watching the farm girl. The sun danced on the water as she washed their flapping ears, and glistened on the buffaloes' skins, turning them shining black.

23

Preeta waved. "Greetings!" She waded out of the water and squatted down on the shore at a respectful distance.

"So! You're a friend of princes!" cried Kanu sarcastically. "You behave as if they were your brothers, always hanging around. Huh!"

Preeta bowed her head uncertainly. "Only if they request my company," she replied modestly.

"I think I should warn you that you're playing with fire. Indeed, Prince Vasu is already beginning to wonder about you; he thinks you're only his friend for what you can get out of him, and that you and his brothers are ganging up against him."

"WHAT?" Preeta was aghast. "He can't possibly think that. He knows I would give my life for him."

"Princes can be very touchy about these things. Next time you see him you'll probably notice he's not so friendly." And tossing a pebble into the water, Kanu strolled away.

Preeta watched the ripples spreading outwards, thinking how it only takes one stone cast in still water to make ripples.

The day before the party, Kanu and Vasu went into the forest to practise archery and came upon Preeta and the younger princes clustered together beneath a tree.

"See what I mean?" hissed Kanu. "They're at it again. Plotting something against you. And that Preeta's in on it. Hey you! Girl!" yelled Kanu. "Think you're a princess in the making, I have no doubt," he sneered. "But no amount of consorting with princes will stop you being only a cow girl."

Preeta leapt to her feet, blushing with misery. "Sire!" she protested, bowing before Prince Vasu. "I would never forget my place."

"Oh, go away!" shouted Vasu angrily, "and don't come back."

With tears streaming down her face, Preeta ran away.

"Why were you so rude to her?" protested Ananta. "What's she done?"

"Why are you being so mean?" demanded Ugra.

But Vasu looked stonily ahead and said nothing.

"You don't seem to see it, Your ROYAL highnesses," sneered Kanu. "You're too trusting. That Preeta – you should watch her. She's such a phoney, sucking up to you all the time, just to see what she can get. Can't you tell?"

"Is that what you think, Vasu?" Ugra angrily asked his oldest brother.

Vasu scowled and swung his brother an unexpected blow, which sent him sprawling. "Remember who's the oldest!" he bellowed.

"Why, you bully! What have I done to deserve that?" howled Ugra, scrambling to his feet and lunging back at Vasu.

"Kanu told me what you're plotting," hissed Vasu.

"WHAT?" exclaimed Ugra, swinging round at Kanu. "What have you been saying about me?"

"Kanu says you want to inherit the kingdom one day," shouted Vasu.

"Liar, liar!" Ugra lunged at Kanu, and Ananta flung himself on Kanu's back, pummelling him furiously. Vasu threw himself on top of all three of them, and they were soon a seething bundle of rolling, punching and kicking.

Fleeing through the forest, Preeta came upon old Sarma. "Please stop them!" she wept. "The princes are fighting. It's that Kanu – he's caused it.

The boys had fought each other to exhaustion when Sarma arrived on the scene.

"Come, come!" Sarma said, easing the princes apart. "The sun is still high. Sit in the shade with me and cool your tempers. What a hullabaloo. What's the trouble? Isn't it better to discuss your problems than fight blindly? It's like the sad tale about the King of the Lions, and a buffalo called Lively. They were such good friends until…"

"We're not good friends. I hate him," snapped Vasu, giving Ugra a last kick before flopping on the ground.

"I hate you too," shouted Ugra, lashing back.

"And he's the worst!" snarled Ananta, giving Kanu a push.

"Boys, boys. Here, help me eat this." Sarma drew a pomegranate from within the folds of his garment, and cut it open with a knife. "Yes – you can share it between you." He tossed a gleaming portion to each boy. "King Lion and the Buffalo were such good and trusty friends, but it all came to a tragic end – because of a treacherous jackal. It's so hard, when you're a prince, to know who your real friends are, isn't it?" Old Sarma cocked his head with a knowing look.

Vasu scowled, only remembering the things Kanu had told him.

"It's about the estrangement of friends," said Sarma so softly that the princes had to edge even closer to hear what he was saying.

King Lion's Friend

How beautiful friendship is;
But beware the treacherous jackal
Who, eaten up by greed,
Will hack it down.

Agreat and noble lion king ruled a forest: a wondrous place full of flowering trees, where all sorts of beasts and creatures lived. King Lion reigned so wisely, and was so well loved, that no one feared him and he feared no one.

It was dawn when King Lion went down to the pool to drink, but suddenly the air was shaken by a thunderous bellow. Never had the forest heard such a sound, and the animals raised their heads in terror. King Lion was paralysed with uncertainty, as wave upon wave of bellows shattered the air. What should he do?

This apprehension was noticed by two layabout jackals called Wily and Wary, sons of two of the king's ministers.

"Hah!" cried Wily. "Look at them all – dithering like frightened mice. This could be an opportunity to offer my services to the king."

"What on earth makes you think he'd want to have anything to do with such a lazy jackal as you?" sneered his friend Wary. "You've not bothered to attend court for ages."

"Well, maybe the time has come to make myself useful," said Wily. So Wily sidled before the anxious king with much bowing and scraping and said, "Sire, I believe I can help you."

"What makes you think that?" asked the king suspiciously.

"I believe you are worried about the terrifying sounds coming from the forest, eh?"

"You're quite right," the king blurted out. "In fact, I'm thinking of moving my kingdom away. If those bellows are anything to go by, that must be some mighty and fearsome creature...." He stopped, ashamed that he had displayed weakness – cowardice even?

"Ah, my lord!" Wily agreed, his voice soft with sympathy. "Why not send me to find out what it is?"

"No, no! It is my duty to investigate. After all, I am king. I should set an example to my people, and show them that I am brave enough to face this unknown creature."

But Wily said, "Sire! No one would expect the king to put himself in danger. Send me and my friend Wary."

The king uneasily gave his permission.

Full of swaggering confidence to hide their own anxiety, Wily and Wary sauntered off in the direction of the bellowing sounds.

"You must be the world's biggest idiot," muttered Wary, feeling faint with fear. "And I must be an even bigger one to follow you."

"Shut up," retorted Wily. "At least look like a warrior even if you are just a snivelling coward."

The bellowing and crashing got closer. Creeping almost on their bellies, the two friends peered through the undergrowth, hoping their chattering teeth wouldn't give them away. And then they saw it! There in the clearing: a huge, white bullock with powerful shoulders, sporting a magnificent hump, looking as glorious as the god Shiva's own bull.

"A bull! It's just a bull!" laughed Wary with relief.

"Oh my," chortled Wily, rolling on his back and kicking his feet in the air. "The king will feel silly."

But Wily's brain was working fast. He sat on his haunches with a cunning look. "I think we can get something out of this," he murmured. "We can't allow the king to lose face, of course, but you know how the world works; peace and friendship followed by war and enmity? I think I can get King Lion just where I want him!"

The two jackals went back to the king, and Wily spun him such a story. "The bellows," he declared, "come from no less a creature than

Lord Shiva's bull prancing in the meadow! The Great God himself has given his bull permission to play in your forest."

King Lion trembled with awe; a sacred beast here in his own forest! "What did you say to him?" he asked Wily.

"I said he had trespassed into the domain of King Lion, the very lion belonging to our beloved Goddess Durga herself."

King Lion was thrilled and flattered. "Well said!" he cried, congratulating Wily. "Go and bring him to me. Give him safe conduct."

So Wily and Wary returned to the bullock. "Hey, Lively!" (That was the bullock's name.) "Although you have been trespassing in the forest of King Lion, for which the penalty could be exceedingly severe, the king has asked to meet you. We'll take you, but listen to a bit of sound advice: don't go getting ideas above yourself. Don't forget who arranged all this. Remember what me and my friend here have done for you. Take your orders from us, show us respect, then all three of us will do all right. His majesty's royal favour will suit us all! Eh?"

"Sounds good to me," sighed the bullock happily. After all, fine creature as he was, in the past he had been merely a beast of burden, sadly abandoned in the forest after he collapsed beneath a heavy load. He was not at all averse to enjoying some royal benefits.

From the moment they met, King Lion and Lively the Bull got on like a house on fire. For once, King Lion felt he was with an equal; he admired Lively's noble strength, and witty conversation. And Lively was much impressed by the king's massive paws and lethal claws.

King Lion showed him all the wonders of the forest: the safest place to bathe, where he wouldn't be attacked by crocodiles, and the coolest glades to shelter from the fiery sun. In return, Lively told him of all the places he'd seen on his travels, and seemed to have such superior wisdom and knowledge that King Lion came to rely on his good advice. They spent so much time together that they had no time for Wily and Wary.

Wily was furious. Things were not going according to plan. After all, wasn't it he who had introduced Lively to King Lion? Where were the royal favours they were supposed to enjoy?

Wily complained bitterly to Wary. "Look at us! We have become thin and hollow-bellied with hunger. King Lion has forgotten us, and Lively only thinks about having fun. We've got to do something."

"It was all your fault in the first place. You introduced them, so you think of something," grumbled Wary.

"I must break up this beautiful friendship between the king and Lively," muttered Wily.

Wily's moment came early one evening. The king had just consumed a whole gazelle and was looking for a quiet place to sleep it off.

Wary watched as Wily slunk slyly towards the royal beast, his vast golden body stretched out beneath the cool shade of a tree.

"Sire! I beseech a word in your ear," Wily called in grave, compelling tones. " I have very serious news for you."

King Lion raised his great head, barely recognising the scrawny jackal before him. "Oh, it's you, Wily. Speak up then, but make it quick. I'm having my afternoon nap."

"It's about Lively the bull," confided Wily. "Ever since I introduced you, you've become best friends, and you confide in him more than your own counsellors. But I have learned something terrible. He's a fraud. He lied. He's not Lord Shiva's bull after all."

"What?" roared King Lion in consternation. "I don't believe it."

"What's more," continued Wily, relishing the impact his words were having, "his heart is full of treachery. Despite all the power and trust you have given him, he still isn't satisfied. In fact he won't ever be satisfied till he has everything. My Lord, don't forget: Lively the bull is a grass-eater, and you, oh mighty king, are a flesh-eater. There can never be true trust when one is merely food for the other."

The king groaned in great distress. "I can't bear to think ill of so good a friend. I need proof."

"You will have proof before your own eyes," declared Wily. "The next time you see Lively, just watch the manner in which he will come before you. He will be slow and hesitant, sidling with lowered gaze and scraping hoof. And why? Because he is riddled with treachery and scheming."

Leaving a sad and thoughtful king, Wily sped into the forest to look for Lively. He came upon him happily grazing on the banks of the river. Wily flopped down in the shade, resting his nose upon his paws.

"Hail, good sire. Fine day!" bellowed the bull good-naturedly.

"I don't think so," answered Wily solemnly.

"Why?" cried Lively. "What makes you so glum?"

"I don't know if you want to hear this," muttered Wily.

"Come, come! Tell me what's bothering you."

"Honoured sir, if I tell you, it's only for your own good. Believe me, I take no pleasure in what I've recently learned. The fact is..."

"Yes?"

"The fact is, the king..."

"Yes?"

"The Great Lord of all the beasts in the forest, is thinking of killing you, and sharing your flesh with all the beasts of prey."

"WHAT?" Lively the bull was astounded. "It can't be true. We are the very best of friends. What on earth could I have done to upset him?"

"Kings can be very touchy, you know. They see offence in the slightest thing. And of course, a grass-eater should never trust a meat-eater."

"But he and I are so close. We discuss everything; I would know if such a thought had ever occurred to him. I don't believe it. I won't believe it. I need proof."

"You will have proof before your very eyes," whispered Wily. "You know King Lion has a favourite rock where he likes to stretch himself out after a meal? Go and meet him, but notice that this time he will be crouched in the hunting position; his tail will be taut, his ears pricked, his eyes suspicious. Beware, I tell you! He is getting bored with eating lean gazelles, and beginning to find your plump flesh irresistible."

"Huh!" spluttered Lively, reeling in outrage. "Just because I am a grass-eater, let no one think I'm not also a mighty enemy," and he swung his head back and forth menacingly.

Wary felt uncomfortable with Wily's game. "Why break up a beautiful friendship? Why sow pain in this life, when we all die in the end, and are reduced to worms and ashes?" he asked his friend.

"Wary, this is statecraft. All statecraft is crooked. You are too simple," argued Wily. "We jackals must look after ourselves by any means possible. If Lively is killed, just think how much meat he will provide for all us meat-eaters!"

Meanwhile, the bull was in an agony of indecision. What should he do? Creep away from King Lion's kingdom? But he might encounter other fierce beasts in the forest and he wouldn't have the king's protection. Whatever he had done to offend the king had been done innocently.

"I'll beg his pardon! Throw myself on his mercy," thought Lively. So Lively went, bowed down with sadness, in search of the king.

The royal lion was stretched full-length across his favourite rock when Lively approached looking hesitant and dejected, just as Wily had said.

"Huh! Here he is, pretending to come in peace. Thinks he can fool me," thought the king, watching through narrowed eyes as the bull drew closer, his head low as if full of scheming thoughts.

As Wily had predicted, the Lion King rose on to his haunches in spring position. His tail stuck out behind him, taut and straight, his ears pricked, his eyes glinted and his muscles braced, ready to pounce.

"No, wait, my Lord! There's some mistake…" Lively howled.

But Lion King had seen his proof. His friend had betrayed him. With one great bound, he hurled himself at Lively, his lightning claws tearing into the bull's body. Bellowing with anger, Lively flung him off and speared his sharp horns into the lion's belly. The king reeled backwards in agony.

For hours the bloody battle went on, each hell-bent on destroying the other. The animals of the forest watched in confusion, some fleeing in despair.

"Oh, Wily, you miserable wretch," cried Wary in horror. "Look what you've done: torn apart a true friendship for some paltry gain of your own, and brought chaos to the forest. Where once we dwelt in peace and harmony, your evil plans have destroyed everything. Oh, why did the king listen to your weasly words? Why did I not stop you? Alas, we are all at fault."

One last terrible bellow rent the forest air, then all was silent. Wily and Wary crept forward.

There was King Lion, bloodied and torn, weeping over the corpse of his beloved Lively. "Alas, alas!
What have I done?

33

Killed my dearest friend, and in slaying him, all I have done is hurt myself."

After many piteous tears, King Lion crept away. In his heart, he knew that it was all because he had listened to a treacherous jackal. Had he been a wiser king, he would have thought things through, listened to an old and trusted friend, and sought for reconciliation before war.

"But it is so hard for a king to know who is a real friend and who is just a scheming jackal," concluded Sarma sorrowfully.

Prince Vasu was up at dawn on the day of his birthday. His servants dressed him in all his blazing finery for a royal procession.

A decorated elephant was waiting, and he was seated in a gold-lined howdah, among velvet cushions, beneath the scarlet shade of a fringed umbrella. Warriors bearing spears ran alongside, with bands of musicians playing pipes and drums, and clashing cymbals.

The people of the kingdom lined the streets, waving and shouting, while Prince Vasu flung gold coins into the crowd.

After the feasting, Ugra and Ananta whispered to their brother, "Come, Vasu! We have a special birthday surprise. Come to the forest."

Vasu frowned. Was this a trick? What if Kanu was right? Would they harm him, perhaps kill him? He hesitated.

Then old Sarma said, "Go, sire, go! I'll come too with your cousin Kanu. Eh?" He glanced at the cousin glowering in a corner.

In an open glade lit by little clay dishes of flickering lights, cushions were spread in readiness for them, and a special big one for Vasu beneath a canopy of turquoise silk draped from the trees.

Ugra waved a hand. A drum began to beat, bells began to ring. From out of the darkness came children: they were tumblers and acrobats; fire-eaters and contortionists. They performed amazing tricks, leaping on each other's backs — three, four, five of them at a time. They swung like monkeys and sprang like deer. Finally they made a huge, human pyramid, and a girl — it was Preeta — ran out and climbed to the top. She stood on the shoulders of the highest acrobats, and began to sing a song of praise to Prince Vasu.

"Haiya Vasu! Great Vasu! We greet you on your birthday!"

"Are you pleased, brother?" asked Ananta with shining eyes. "Do you like your secret present?"

Suddenly all was clear. Prince Vasu bowed his head in shame.

"That's all we were doing," whispered Ugra to his older brother, "planning a surprise for you."

"You shouldn't believe everything you hear," murmured old Sarma, as Kanu crept away, "especially when you're told it by a jackal."

Her Weight in Gold

With the Royal Archery Contest coming up, there was much excitement and practice going on throughout the kingdom. Princes and warriors from far and wide were taking part, all keen to win a fabulous prize – the winner's weight in gold.

Every late afternoon when the heat was waning, Preeta watched her friends, Princes Vasu and Ugra, practising their archery, while she and the youngest prince, Ananta, were on hand to fetch and carry their arrows. After sunset, Preeta returned to her hut in the village and told her widowed mother of all the exploits they had been up to: their rivalries, jealousies and expectations. "The prize is the winner's weight in gold!"

"Goodness," sighed her mother. "Even the weight of your little hand in gold would provide you with a dowry without putting us into debt for generations. If only I had a son who could enter and win."

"Even if you did, mother, he'd be no use," Preeta reminded her patiently. "This contest is only for warriors and princes, not farm boys!"

"Well then, he could have won you a buffalo at the village contest - but that can't happen either."

Mmm... thought Preeta rebelliously. Who says? A girl she might be, but her father had taught her archery before he died, and she knew no boys in the village who were better than her. Why shouldn't she try and win the buffalo? She and her mother only owned a few goats and chickens. It was other people's buffaloes she minded every day.

Plans formed in her mind. When she drove the village buffaloes down to the river, she always took her bow and arrows with her in case she was confronted by a leopard or tiger. But now she had another purpose: to enter the village competition and win the prize of a buffalo.

Most of the village boys had rough, home-made bows, but Preeta's bow was different. Her father had made it specially for her, and she thought it the best bow in the world. It may not have been carved, lacquered and edged with gold like the royal bows, but it was made from the finest bamboo. And when she fitted her arrow, with its hawk feathers and tip made from buffalo bone, it bent with incredible power and strength as she pulled back the string, ready for action.

Preeta pinned a piece of animal skin to a tree as a target and began to practise, while her buffaloes wandered along the river bank. She heard her father's words in her head. "If only you were a boy, one day you would outshoot every warrior in the land."

That afternoon, Prince Ugra was feeling out of sorts with the world: he had quarrelled violently with his brothers and felt nothing but jealousy when the two of them had gone off boating without him.

Vasu was better than him at everything, though only a little better than him at archery. "If only I could beat Vasu in the archery contest!" he thought. Mounting a horse, Ugra rode into the forest with his bow and arrows, looking for a quiet glade to practise.

Rounding the river bank he spotted Preeta on the other side. What was she up to? She had a crude bow and arrows, and seemed to be practising. Again and again she hit the target right in the middle, each time stepping further back. What strength of bow, and perfect eye!

Ugra frowned. How could a mere farmer's girl be so good an archer?

"You're not bad!" he finally called out. "Good enough to compete in the royal contest."

Preeta turned, startled. She put her hands together and bowed respectfully. "Even if I were able to take part, I'd be nowhere near good enough to compete against Your Lordship. But I have a good bow. My father made it for me. He was an excellent archer, and always won the contests in the village."

"Bring it to me," said Ugra, dismounting. There was an old log, fallen across the river, which was used as a bridge. Preeta crossed nimbly to the other side and obediently held out her bow for the prince to see.

Ugra took the bow in his hands as if it were his right.

Preeta was suddenly full of anxiety. She knew the laws of courtesy. If the prince desired her bow, she would be obliged to give it to him.

"This is a wonderful bow," Ugra murmured enviously. He examined the pliable bend of the wood, and felt it spring in his hands. " With such a bow, I could beat even my brother, Vasu. I wish it were mine."

"Then, my Lord, if that is what you wish, the bow is yours," said Preeta with breaking heart. Without her bow, she couldn't even dream of entering the village contest. Her brain raced. What could she do?

"I am pleased," nodded Ugra, slinging the bow over his shoulder and mounting his horse.

"But, Your Highness," Preeta cried desperately. "May I respectfully point out that my bow is too small for you. It was made specially for me, and you are much taller than I. My father's bow hangs above our doorway. I think that would suit you better."

Ugra paused. It was true, Preeta was smaller than him. "Very well," he said. "Fetch your father's bow. I'll return to the river just before sunset, and wait for you at the log. I'll see which bow suits me best."

Preeta watched him go, but instead of relief, she felt even more anxious. She was in a proper pickle, for though she hadn't lied, she had failed to mention that her father's bow had a fine, almost invisible crack – which might split at any time. They had only kept the bow in memory of him. Gloomily, she crossed back over the river and drove her buffaloes home.

By the time she had finished her chores, the sun was just beginning to gild the tops of the trees. She took down the cracked bow which hung over the doorway and hurried back to the river.

Ugra was already there. He slid from his horse. "Ah! Good. Have you got your father's bow? Bring it to me."

Preeta stood transfixed with terror. What had she done? She would never get away with this deception. The minute Ugra tried out her father's old bow, he would know he'd been cheated. Slowly, as in a dream, she walked the log across the river and handed over the bow.

Ugra seemed pleased at first; he pulled back the string, flexed the wood, and felt its strength and pliability. Selecting an arrow from the sheath, he fitted it to the string and let fly.

"You're right. This suits me better," he said. "You may have yours back."

"Thank you," whispered Preeta, taking her bow and flying back across the log. But she no sooner reached the other side when she heard a terrible crack. Ugra had fitted another arrow and pulled the string back and back until the bow was bent almost double and, as he let fly, it snapped, and the bow broke into two.

Ugra looked in consternation at the two pieces, and then he saw the fine crack in each half. "Why, you witch!" he yelled. "You tricked me. This bow was cracked. You must have known. Give me back your bow."

Preeta had noticed before that the log over the river was beginning to rot, but it had always carried her weight. She knew it was unworthy, but she had one last desperate hope. "I'm afraid to cross the river again, I think the log is rotten."

Ugra was outraged. "What lies! Trying to get away with it, are you? I'll get it myself then." And the prince stepped on to the log.

For a moment he paused, watching the river swirling underneath, and strode across the log. But as he reached halfway, there was a shuddering creak. Snap! With a piercing cry, he plunged into the river.

The prince surfaced, gulping and yelling. "Help! I can't swim!"

Filled with remorse, Preeta flung herself into the river to save him.

Sarma always went walking with his pupils each evening before sunset. But there was no sign of Ugra. Someone had seen the prince riding towards the river, so they followed. They heard the cry and the splash, and dashed to the water's edge to see Ugra and Preeta thrashing about in the water.

"You treacherous little vixen," he was shouting. "You tricked me, didn't you! I'll have you whipped for this!"

" I'm sorry, I'm sorry!" she wept, as she helped him back to the bank.

"Excuse me, my lord." It was old Sarma. "Can I help solve anything?"

Ugra pointed a furious finger at Preeta. "She tried to drown me."

"I didn't mean it!" she stammered. "I just wanted my bow back."

Later, as they sat shamefacedly in fresh, dry clothes, the whole story spluttered out.

Preeta confessed. "I wanted to enter the village contest and win a buffalo to add to my dowry. But I needed my own bow," she wept. "Prince Ugra has a dozen bows to choose from. I only have the one my father made for me, and His Highness wanted it."

"Hmmmm..." pondered Sarma. "It reminds me of the story of the Ape and the Crocodile, and how important it is to value what you've got, and not always want what others have...."

The Ape and the Crocodile

A beauteous rose-apple tree grew on the banks of a broad river, its branches always laden with fruit. An ape called Red Face lived in this tree, bounding among the apples in endless bliss, never needing to go anywhere else for food.

A crocodile called Hideous Jaws swam beneath the tree one day, and climbed up on to the silvery shore to bask in the shade. Red Face noticed him and said, "As a visitor to my shore, please allow me the honour of presenting you with a gift of this divine fruit."

The crocodile accepted most gratefully, and the two of them sat long into the afternoon, talking happily like old friends. After that, Hideous Jaws came to visit Red Face nearly every day, and each time Red Face gave his friend rosy apples to take back to his wife. But the wife was curious to know where these apples came from.

"My Lord, " she said one day, "where do you get such glorious fruit?"

"I have a dear friend," said her husband, "an ape called Red Face, whose tree it is. He always insists that I bring you some of his rosy apples."

The crocodile wife sighed. "Anyone who eats only the food of the gods must have a heart of ambrosia. If you love me, bring me the heart of this ape so that we can eat it together, and both gain eternal youth and everlasting life."

"Oh no! I couldn't possibly!" cried Hideous Jaws, aghast. "Red Face is my friend and sworn brother. That's a horrible desire."

But the crocodile wife whined and moaned. "I believe this ape is a female," she accused him, "and you're besotted with her. That's why you spend the whole day across the river, neglecting me."

"No! How can you say that?" protested Hideous Jaws.

"It's true. You love another, and if you don't fetch me her heart, I shall starve myself to death."

Hideous Jaws was utterly miserable. What could he do? If he didn't kill Red Jaws and bring his heart to her, she would die from starvation, and his first loyalty must surely be to his wife.

For a while he couldn't bring himself to visit Red Face, but true to her word, his wife stubbornly refused to eat. Finally, seeing she was on the point of death, he swam across the river trying to think how he could obtain Red Face's heart.

"Welcome! Long time no see," the ape called from the branches of

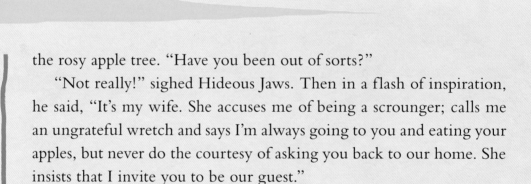

the rosy apple tree. "Have you been out of sorts?"

"Not really!" sighed Hideous Jaws. Then in a flash of inspiration, he said, "It's my wife. She accuses me of being a scrounger; calls me an ungrateful wretch and says I'm always going to you and eating your apples, but never do the courtesy of asking you back to our home. She insists that I invite you to be our guest."

"How kind of her!" exclaimed Red Face. "The surest sign of affection and friendship is to give and receive, to speak and to listen, to feed and to be fed. Sadly, I am a forest dweller and, as much as I would be honoured to receive your hospitality, your home is in the water. How can I possibly go there?"

"See that sandbank across the water? It isn't far, and I can easily carry you there on my back," said Hideous Jaws persuasively.

"Brilliant! What a good idea. I am ready to go!" And Red Face leapt down from his tree and, trustingly, sat astride the crocodile's back.

42

Hideous Jaws lashed his tail, and they were soon zooming across the waters at great speed.

"Hey! Not so fast, good friend," pleaded Red Face. "I'm getting thoroughly soaked, and I'm afraid I'll fall in and drown."

'Ah!' thought Hideous Jaws. 'Red Face is terrified of water. He is in my power. Now is the moment to reveal my true intentions, and at least, give him a chance to make his peace with God.'

Red Face was aghast when he heard how Hideous Jaws had tricked him. "I thought you were my friend," he wailed piteously. "Tell me, brother, what harm have I ever done to you and your wife, that you should want to kill me?"

"I'm afraid it's because of your luscious fruit," sighed the crocodile apologetically. "My wife is convinced that the rosy apples in your tree are the food of the gods; the source of everlasting life. And as you eat nothing but rosy apples, then your heart too must be pure ambrosia. She wants to eat your heart and live for ever in youth and beauty. So sadly, my friend, I must kill you, for my first duty is to my wife."

Now it was Red Face who had a good idea. "Dear brother! Why on earth didn't you say so from the start? I would have brought the real heart of ambrosia with me. My own heart is worthless. The true heart is concealed in a hollow of my tree. Turn round! Take me back, so that I can fetch it for you."

The crocodile was overjoyed. He had never wanted to kill Red Face. "Thank Goodness! Now we can give my wife the true heart, and you and I can still be friends." Turning round, he returned to the tree with the rosy apples, and the ape silently sent up thousands of thankful prayers to the gods.

Red Face leapt from the crocodile's back, scampered to the very top of the tree and sat with beating heart, unable to believe his narrow escape.

Hideous Jaws called out impatiently. "Hey, Red Face! Why are you taking so long? Let's get this sweet heart back to my wife, before she starves to death."

"You treacherous creature! I'm not coming down — not after what you've done. Just because she's your wife, doesn't mean you have to do everything she asks, and it certainly doesn't mean that you should go killing your friends, just because she says so."

The crocodile was deeply ashamed. "Please forgive me."

Just then, a little fish swam up to the crocodile. "Hideous Jaws! Something terrible's happened. Another crocodile has taken over your house and killed your wife."

"Oh woe!" wept Hideous Jaws. "Now I've lost everything: my house, my wife and my best friend." He turned to Red Face pitifully. "Dear old friend, remember that seven paces makes a friendship, and we have walked more than seven paces together. Forgive me, and tell me what to do?"

"My advice," said Red Face, feeling just a little sorry for him, "is to go home! Fight for your house, and get back your dignity. And in future, enjoy what you have, and live in peace."

So Hideous Jaws returned home. He kicked out the intruder,

recovered his house, and learned to be satisfied with what he had.

As for Red Face, he continued to bound among the branches of his rosy apple tree, and resolved to be more careful in future with whom he made friends.

Only a fool lets himself be coaxed
Into parting with what is his;
Only a nitwit lets himself be tricked,
As the crocodile tricked the ape.

"But who was the fool in this case?" asked Vasu. "Preeta or my brother, Ugra?"

Sarma sighed. "It is the job of princes to understand their people, and to make wise decisions on their behalf. If a prince acts improperly, what can he expect of his people?"

"As I am responsible for Prince Ugra nearly drowning, I will give him my bow," said Preeta. "It's all I can do to make amends."

"No, Preeta," replied Ugra, getting to his feet. "Your bow is too small for me. It was made especially for you and, as you reminded me, I have many bows. But I wouldn't mind a few lessons from you."

On the day of the Royal Contest, Ugra could not beat his brother, Vasu – but neither did his brother beat him. They were so equally matched that both shared the prize, each sitting on the scales, and each awarded half their weight in gold.

And as for Preeta, even though people whispered with disapproval, the village elders allowed her to enter the village contest. With the bow her father made for her, she easily won the buffalo. How proudly Preeta led it home to her mother to keep for her dowry.

"You may not be a son," smiled her mother proudly, "but to me, you're worth your weight in gold."

Ruby Eye

Every morning, Prince Ananta loved to waken to the sound of the family of monkeys who lived in the forest just beyond the palace gardens. His brothers jeered when he told them that the monkeys were his friends. He had even given them names: Long Tail, Ruby Eye, Silk Fur and Light Finger.

His favourite was Ruby Eye. Prince Ananta had watched him ever since he was born. He had seen him clinging upside-down to his mother's breast as she swung from branch to branch and, when Ruby Eye was older, go bounding among the branches with his brothers and sisters. One day, he leapt right on to Ananta's balcony, and sat on the marble rail, gazing at the prince with his ruby eyes. That's when Ananta named him Ruby Eye.

"Ruby Eye's my best friend," Ananta would tell everyone.

His brothers mocked him, calling him "Monkey Face" or "Flea Bag"! But Ananta took no notice and left his monkey fruit, nuts, vegetables and chapattis on his balcony.

His nurse upbraided him. "Sire, look at the mess!" she groaned, calling in a servant yet again to sweep up the nut shells and banana skins.

How Ananta longed to join the monkeys, especially when they swung away into the forest canopy, sometimes disappearing for days and weeks, while he waited impatiently for their return.

On Ananta's birthday his mother gave him a golden monkey hanging from a golden chain. It had a diamond for its nose, and rubies for eyes.

"It's my Ruby Eye!" he shouted with pleasure, and announced he would wear it forever.

The only time he took off his golden monkey was at bedtime, and he hung it from the bedpost where he could see it the moment he woke up.

One morning, the sound of chattering echoed among the trees. Ananta leapt out of bed with a shout of joy. "They're back!"

Ruby Eye sat on the balcony rail and stretched out his thin, leathery fingers, as if saying, "Glad to see you! Now what have you got for me?"

Ananta grabbed a handful of apples and bananas from the fruit bowl. "I'm so glad you're back," he cried, tossing Ruby Eye an apple. "You missed my birthday, but I kept some treats just for you," and he ran in and out, bringing forth all sorts of delicious nibbles.

"Look what my mother gave me." Ananta showed Ruby Eye the golden monkey. "It reminds me of you. I wear it every day!"

His brothers, whose bedchambers were on the floor above, leaned over their balconies mocking him. "You must have been a monkey in your past life, you're smelly enough! Has Ayah checked you for fleas recently?"

Then Ugra whispered, "Vasu! Let's play a trick on Ananta. Let's hide his golden monkey, and pretend his monkey friend took it! That'll be a laugh." They chortled with glee.

Ananta was already deeply asleep when Ugra and Vasu crept into his bedchamber that night. The golden monkey was hanging from the bedpost. Ugra kept a look-out, while Vasu soundlessly lifted the chain over the bedknob. To make it look more convincing, they scattered a few peanuts on the floor, and placed an apple by the balcony before creeping out again. Back in their chambers they cackled like hyenas, impatient to see Ananta's reaction.

The next morning, what a hullaballoo! Ananta was yelling and shouting, "Where's my monkey!" Accusations flew around. "Someone must have stolen it," he cried.

The servants quaked with anxiety, knowing that if any of them were thought responsible, it would mean a lashing and instant dismissal. Ananta had already grabbed a cane and was whirling it round.

Ayah rushed in. "Sire! I beg you, calm yourself and tell us what has happened."

"Someone has stolen my golden monkey," raged Ananta. "I hung it from the bedpost as usual, last night, and when I woke up this morning it was gone. It didn't walk by itself. Someone's taken it." And he turned on his servant.

The unfortunate man fell to his knees, denying everything, but Ananta showered him with blows until old Sarma arrived and pulled the young prince into his arms. "Ananta! Calm yourself. This is no way to get at the truth."

"The trouble with Ananta is, he's so in love with his monkeys he can't see what's obvious!" sneered Prince Vasu.

"Yes!" agreed Ugra. "Look!" He pointed to the monkey nuts scattered on the floor. "And look!" He pointed to the apple lying on the balcony.

"It was your friends, the monkeys! I bet you anything your beloved Ruby Eye stole it, dirty little thief!"

"All monkeys are thieves. Let's get'em!" And Vasu hurtled outside, followed by the entire household. They grabbed sticks and stones and, gathering round the tree, pelted the monkeys.

In a desperate bid for safety, Ruby Eye leapt from the tree on to the balcony, balancing nervously on the rail as all sorts of objects were flung at him from below.

"Ruby Eye!" Ananta cried furiously, running forward. "How could you? I was your friend." And he hurled an apple at the animal.

The apple struck Ruby Eye right in the forehead, and the monkey plunged to the stone terrace below.

Ananta leaned over, distraught and weeping, then rushed down and knelt beside the lifeless creature. "I'm sorry, I'm sorry! But why did you do it? I thought you were my friend."

Suddenly, a quiet voice said, "Is this what you're looking for?"

Old Sarma came forward, the golden monkey dangling from his fingers, while Vasu and Ugra peered shamefacedly from behind him.

"Sorry, Ananta!" they murmured. "We took it – for a joke."

Horror spread over Ananta's face as he realised the truth.

He snatched the golden monkey, and threw it far into the deep grass of the forest. "I don't want it. I hate you!" wept Ananta. "You've made me kill my friend."

Later, old Sarma took the princes for a walk in the gardens. Ananta trailed behind, refusing to be anywhere near his brothers or say anything to them, except to denounce them as thieves and murderers.

"Yes," said Sarma gently. "They stole your monkey as a bad joke, but it is you, Ananta, who killed your friend. People, especially princes, should consider their every act with the utmost care, and consider the consequences. Before you jump to conclusions, before acting rashly, before you give in to bitter remorse – which solves nothing – listen to a story about the wife and her pet mongoose."

The Faithful Mongoose

There was once a Brahmin and his wife who longed for a baby. While waiting in hope, offering prayers and gifts to the gods, the wife befriended a female mongoose. Every day, she left out a saucer of milk for the friendly creature.

At last, the wife found she was going to have a baby, and was overjoyed. But she didn't forget the female mongoose. She always left her milk, and delighted in seeing her faithful friend.

When her time came, the wife gave birth to a baby boy. At the very same moment the female mongoose gave birth too, but died, leaving her little one wriggling helplessly on the ground.

The horrified wife gathered up the little creature and suckled it at her breast just as she did her own child. Every time she lovingly massaged her baby boy with fine oils, she also massaged the baby mongoose, and reared both with deep affection.

The little mongoose thrived and grew, but the wife never forgot that it was, after all, the creature's instinct to kill, and that perhaps it had been unwise to rear it alongside her baby. So she always kept watch, and never left her baby alone.

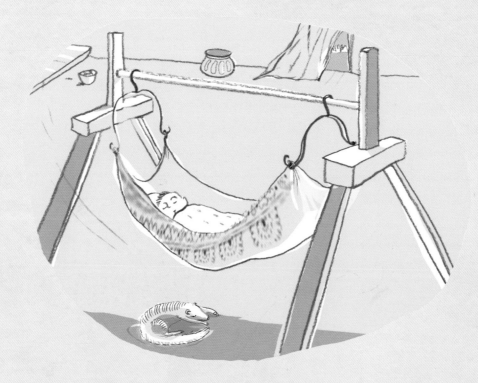

One day, as her little son lay gurgling in his cot, the Brahmin's wife told her husband that she must go and fetch water from the well. On no account must he leave their baby unattended. The husband promised faithfully so, reassured, she took up her water pot on her head and set off for the well.

After a while, the Brahmin felt hungry. His son was fast asleep, so he thought he would go out, just for a little while, to beg for alms. Collecting his bowl and staff, he went to the temple, leaving the house empty except for the little mongoose curled up on the baby's quilt.

As fate would have it, a poisonous serpent slithered out of a hole and headed straight for the baby's cot. The little mongoose reared up protectively. Not only was he determined to save the baby, the snake was his most deadly enemy, and it was in his nature to fight it.

He sprang from the cot and met the serpent halfway across the floor. A terrible battle ensued. The snake writhed and whipped its powerful body this way and that, and the little creature ripped into its skin with bared teeth, avoiding the serpent's poisonous fangs. At last the mongoose gripped the snake by its neck and killed it.

The mongoose was elated. What a hero the baby's mother would think him! How proud of him she would be for saving her baby's life! He heard her singing as she returned home, and rushed out to meet her.

When the Brahmin's wife saw her pet mongoose running towards her, its fur ragged and its jaws dripping with blood, she gave a dreadful scream. "The vicious little beast has killed my baby!" And she dropped her heavy, brimming water pot on top of the little animal, killing it instantly.

Full of terror, she ran into the house. Scattered across the floor were the bloody remnants of the serpent, while chuckling, safe and happy in his cot, was her beloved son.

She fell to her knees with a grief-stricken wail, beating her head and breast with remorse. "What have I done?"

The Brahmin returned and, thinking the worst, rushed in full of guilt. "Dearest wife! What has happened?"

She turned on him, distraught. "Why did you leave our son alone? Shame on you! Shame, shame! Just because you couldn't bear a little hunger. You thought only of your own desires, and left our baby in danger. Now I have killed this innocent mongoose, whom I loved as dearly as my own baby – and who defended our child with its life."

Old Sarma ended the story.

Ananta was weeping quietly, and his brothers sat with bowed heads. It was just a prank, they protested over and over again. But they all understood. Ananta had loved his gold monkey and his real monkey, but in a moment of anger he had destroyed them both.

A man – even a prince who should know better – can perform a rash and dreadful deed. And though it may be because of a misunderstanding or pitiless fate, yet the whole world will condemn it.

Treachery

When Prince Kanu next came to visit, Preeta saw something different about the royal cousin: he looked more like a man and less like a boy; he had the beginnings of a moustache, and always carried a sword at his belt.

She noticed he spent less time with his younger cousins Vasu, Ugra and Ananta, though they too had grown. Vasu, also with a whisper of a moustache above his lip, was less arrogant and more thoughtful. Ugra, no longer jealous of his brothers, had become a peacemaker, keeping the balance between the two. Ananta had lost his baby plumpness and stopped his tantrums and had become kinder and less selfish. All of them were more able to talk to each other without squabbling and fighting.

However, Kanu was still trying to sabotage old Sarma's teachings and lure the princes away. But Sarma would entrance them back with his tales, and Kanu would slink off in disgust.

Of course, it hadn't escaped the old teacher's notice that whenever Prince Kanu was around, things went badly wrong. He was an envious, mistrustful, scheming boy, the kind who loved to trigger conflict and set brother against brother. Sarma knew that this was what rulers had to deal with all the time, and there was no simple solution.

That spring, when Cousin Kanu came to visit, he spent less time with the young princes. He was to be seen riding his white horse across the palace estate, walking the palace walls, sucking the hubble-bubble with the boatmen by the river, and going to the chief counsellor's evening garden house to sip wine.

Kanu's movements would have gone unnoticed, had it not been for Preeta. Preeta had always mistrusted Kanu. She didn't like the condescending way he treated his younger cousins. She didn't like the superior way he treated the palace staff. It was almost as though he thought he owned them.

While guarding the village buffaloes, Preeta would see Kanu riding the grounds of the palace as if inspecting them. She mentioned it to Lakshman the washerman, who mentioned it to Hari the tailor, who mentioned it to Rupit, a manservant of the palace, who mentioned it to Vikram the watchman, who mentioned it to Dilip, a warrior, who repeated it to the Chief of the Army.

"Hmm! There's something fishy about this. Smells like a plot," murmured the army chief. "I must warn the king."

But King Amara Sakti refused to believe that his own kinsman would plot against him. "Kanu's father King Bhoja and I were brought up together like brothers, and Kanu is like a brother to my sons," he insisted.

The army chief increased his surveillance. Everyone agreed that Kanu's behaviour was suspicious. Spies were sent to Kanu's kingdom. Worrying intelligence came back: King Bhoja was plotting to take King Amara Sakti's kingdom by force. Kanu was acting as a spy and sending back detailed information about the layout of the palace and grounds, and where its weak points might be.

On hearing the news, King Amara Sakti sorrowfully summoned his sons, counsellors and advisers.

Some counsellors suggested a meeting between the two kings to make a pact, while others said it would be useless.

Previously, the princes might have shouted vengefully that Kanu should be thrown into a pit of snakes or dumped in a river of crocodiles. But instead, Prince Vasu quietly advised his father to call upon old Sarma for advice.

Sarma listened attentively as everyone vented their rage, then asked, "Sire, have you any idea why your kinsman hates you so much?"

The king reflected sadly, "King Bhoja and I were boys together. When my father died, I went to live with him. We were brought up as brothers, educated together and treated equally. But...." King Amara Sakti hung his head. He remembered how, as a boy, he had bullied Bhoja, had belittled him at every opportunity, always beaten him at archery, was always better at his studies – and had never failed to point it out.

He could still hear his own voice sneering at his cousin. "You're as thick as a plank! Just a dolt!" When they fought each other with fists, it was always he, Amara Sakti, who won.

"When the old king died," King Amara Sakti continued, "I was more popular with the people than Bhoja, and they said they wanted me to be king. But of course Bhoja thought he was entitled to the kingdom. There was a battle. He lost, yet I gave him back part of the kingdom, and I moved my palace here across the river to rule the rest. I longed for us to live in peace. I thought all had been forgiven and forgotten. I always made King Bhoja and his son, Kanu, welcome here. But it seems I was wrong, and all these years he has simply been looking for an opportunity to take my kingdom from me."

King Amara Sakti looked at his three sons standing before him. In a mere six months, with old Sarma as their teacher, they had become worthy enough to be kings. Must he, their father, now bequeath them war and conflict?

King Amara Sakti turned to old Sarma in desperation. "Pray, sir! You are wise. What should I do?"

In a few days Sarma would be leaving the court. His job was done. In just six months, he had transformed the three young princes into thoughtful, wiser and kinder young men.

Yet he knew rulers had to have other qualities too. To protect their kingdoms they must know their enemies; learn when to be ruthless, learn how to combine strength with justice.

Old Sarma knew he had one last, very important story to tell them all: the king, his sons and the court advisers. A story of tough decisions. A lesson for all rulers.

"Sire, listen to my story about the Owls and the Crows. It may help you to decide what to do."

Owls and Crows

Trust not a former enemy
Who comes in friendship.

The King of the Owls could not forget that a long time ago the Owls had been fierce enemies of the Crows. This hatred had been passed on from one generation to the next, and King Owl still killed any Crow who crossed his path.

Indeed, King Owl and his warriors went on nightly killing sprees into Crow territory. Night after night, so many Crows were slaughtered that King Crow called his ministers together. "We can't go on letting King Owl kill us like this," he said. "Have you any suggestions?"

King Crow pondered all the options: should he make peace, go to war, retreat, find friends, or find other powerful allies? He asked all his ministers one by one.

But there was one last minister to consult, called Live Firm. He was a wily, cynical old Crow. He had no belief in anything except what was good for Crows. When King Crow asked his advice he said, "There is another option: trickery."

King Crow was taken aback. "Trickery? But our gods require us to be honest."

"With the gods, yes, we must be honest, and with ourselves, and with our own kind," agreed the old counsellor. "But with our enemies, double-dealing is best. Those who are honest with their foes do not last long. Better to confuse them, offer them first peace, then war. Stir up uncertainty and you will create weakness within their ranks. You can beat your enemies by getting to know them. Animals know their foe by their smell, but monarchs have spies. My advice is that you send secret agents into your enemy's camp. Learn all about him: his plans, his strengths and his weaknesses."

King Crow sighed in distress. "Why do the Owls hate us so much that we have to take these measures?"

But in his heart he knew why. It was all the fault of the Crows in the first place. Generations ago, when the kingdom of birds had been about to anoint the Owl as sovereign, a brainless, trouble-making Crow had flown in and jeered at them for appointing "an ugly old bird".

"Look at him! Blind by day and greedy by night! Cunning he may be, but it's just to satisfy his own appetite. Who would want to be ruled by such a creature?"

Hearing this, all the birds flew away, abandoning the Owls with their king, alone and uncrowned.

The Owls were outraged. "A forest, when hacked down by the axe, may heal and grow again, but let me tell you, oh wretched Crows, the wounds you have inflicted on us will never heal. From now on, there will be enmity between Crows and Owls for ever and ever."

In the silence of the empty forest, King Crow was full of remorse. How stupid to have made an enemy for no reason! Now, facing annihilation, they had no choice but to fight the Owls with everything they had, and if that meant duplicity – then so be it.

Live Firm had a plan. King Crow must pretend he had discovered that his old counsellor was a traitor. He was to fight and bloody him, and have him thrown out of the kingdom.

"How can I do this to you?" wept King Crow.

"Do not pity me. I am old," said Live Firm. "Remember, you are the king: your people are there for you. In times of peace, you nourish and care for them, but in times of war they become like arrows to be fired. That is what they owe you in return. I too am just a weapon for your use. Let the Owls hear you call me a traitor; beat me up, make it look convincing, then fly away as though in retreat. Hurry! For it will soon be night."

So King Crow leapt upon his old counsellor's back. He tore and pecked at his feathers and smeared him with blood. The Crows of his kingdom flew around in alarm. "What's happening?" they cawed.

"I have just discovered that Live Firm is a traitor," shouted King Crow. "He is lucky I do not kill him," and he ejected the old adviser from the tree, sending him crashing to the ground.

An Owl, spying on them from some distance, rushed back to his king. "Sire! The Crows are in disarray. They fight among themselves, and have thrown out their most trusted adviser. Now's the time to wipe them out."

King Owl and his army flew over to find the Crow kingdom in confusion and old Live Firm lying wounded on the ground.

"Help! Look at me!" wailed Live Firm. "Look what a miserable state my own king has reduced me to. Take me before your sovereign. I have something important to tell him."

King Owl saw the terrible state in which Live Firm had been abandoned. "Why did your own kind do this to you?" he exclaimed.

"I tried to stop them going to war with you," stammered Live Firm, lying through his beak. "I told my king that you were too strong, too powerful, that it would be folly for them to fight you. Better to make peace, was my advice. But you know how it is if someone tells you a home truth? You hate them for it. So now they hate me. They will never have me back. Have mercy on me and I swear to serve only you in future."

King Owl turned to his general, Red Eye. "What do you think?"

"Kill the fellow," Red Eye declared. "You know the old saying.

Kill your foe when he is down and at his weakest. Otherwise he'll grow strong again and fight you more powerfully."

But King Owl's other advisers thought differently. "Red Eye is too merciless. This Crow seeks your sanctuary, even though he knows you could make a meal of him. Spare his life and he'll grow to love you, and become a faithful servant. His inside knowledge of Crows could serve our interests."

So King Owl ordered Live Firm to be cared for.

The old Crow groaned cunningly. "Why not let me die? Then perhaps I could be born again as an Owl and truly become one of you noble birds."

Red Eye was not in the least fooled. "You crafty one!" he declared. "Even if you were born again as an Owl, you would never be one of us."

But King Owl was convinced by Live Firm. "Stay in my palace and be treated royally," he said courteously.

"I don't deserve it," intoned the humble Crow. "You have made my body holy from the dust of your feet. I'll serve you better if I live at your gate."

"Huh!" Red Eye was disgusted.

As time passed, he observed the old Crow becoming stronger by the day with all the care and attention he was receiving. "You're a pack of fools!" he accused King Owl's ministers. "Can't you see? You're fattening up your enemy. Beware. He'll turn round and destroy you!"

Now the Owls got really fed up with Red Eye, and completely ignored him.

Red Eye cried out with contempt. "I'm off! I have warned you, but you won't listen. You must face your fate without me. I leave you to your doom!" And Red Eye flew away.

Live Firm was delighted. With Red Eye out of the way, the old Crow could plan the downfall of the Owls. While each night the Owls went on their Crow-killing spree, each day Live Firm cunningly lined his nest with dry firewood. At last, when he felt he had enough wood, he flew off while the Owls were sleeping, to find King Crow.

His sovereign was delighted to see him. "Thank goodness you're well. How have you been getting on?"

"There's no time to lose," urged Live Firm. "You must act now to destroy the Owls. Every Crow must carry a burning twig to my nest in the Owl Fortress. Hurry!"

So King Crow and his citizens each took a twig and, lighting it from a small wayside fire, followed Live Firm back to the Owl Kingdom.

One by one, they dropped their burning twigs into his nest. The fire spread. Soon the whole kingdom was ablaze, and every single, sleepy, sluggish, unsuspecting Owl was slain.

"Only one Owl got away," the old counsellor told King Crow triumphantly. "Their once-oh-so-venerated general Red Eye. He suspected me, but they ignored him – and he left the kingdom. So now, King Crow, you have a chance to rule wisely: to know how to distinguish enemies from friends, when to trust your advisers, and the right time for peace, war, or a truce. The enmity between Crows and Owls is over."

"Finally," said old Sarma as he ended the story, "every king and prince should remember that all earthly things pass; whether beggar or king, Owl or Crow. In the end,

> Gone will be the king,
> Gone his ministers,
> Gone the beautiful queens,
> Gone those glorious woods and groves.
> All must pass away; each lost, each mortally stung by the Great Ender.

King Amara Sakti invited King Bhoja to witness his handing over of the throne to his eldest son, Vasu. There was a grand ceremony and a show of strength. The whole army pledged allegiance to the new king. Ugra and Ananta were also given kingdoms to rule on behalf of their brother, and they too publicly pledged absolute loyalty to Vasu.

Prince Kanu and his father returned to their kingdom knowing that in future they must be allied to King Amara Sakti, and that they would gain far more from friendship than by enmity.

> *The first rule of intelligence*
> *Is to leave alone what is working;*
> *The second rule*
> *Is to complete to the end what has been begun.*

And so Sri Sarma left the court with honour preserved and his job well done. He returned to the forest to spend his last days as a hermit in prayer and penitence.

His wisdom would be his legacy. And though his body would die and crumble to ashes, he would live for ever and beyond in the hearts and minds of the three princes who, for six months, had been his pupils.

▶▶

———————